The Wounded Lion

A TALE FROM SPAIN

Retold by Suzanne I. Barchers
Illustrated by John Joven

RED
CHAIR
·PRESS·

Please visit our website at **www.redchairpress.com**.
Find a free catalog of all our high-quality products for young readers.

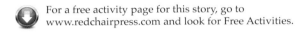

For a free activity page for this story, go to
www.redchairpress.com and look for Free Activities.

The Wounded Lion

Publisher's Cataloging-In-Publication Data
(Prepared by The Donohue Group, Inc.)

Barchers, Suzanne I.
The wounded lion : a tale from Spain / retold by Suzanne I. Barchers ; illustrated by John Joven.
p. : col. ill. ; cm. -- (Tales of honor)
Summary: Day after day, a poor young girl discovers a lion who needs her help. In time, her care for the wounded lion and dreams of a better life intersect in a most unusual way. This Spanish folktale is about perseverance and compassion. Includes special educational sections: Words to know, What do you think?, and About Spain.
Interest age level: 006-010.
ISBN: 978-1-937529-79-6 (lib. binding/hardcover)
ISBN: 978-1-937529-63-5 (pbk.)
ISBN: 978-1-936163-95-3 (eBook)
1. Compassion--Juvenile fiction. 2. Perseverance (Ethics)--Juvenile fiction. 3. Girls--Juvenile fiction.
4. Lion--Juvenile fiction. 5. Folklore--Spain. 6. Compassion--Fiction. 7. Perseverance (Ethics)--Fiction.
8. Girls--Fiction. 9. Lions--Fiction. 10. Folklore--Spain. I. Joven, John. II. Title.

PZ8.1.B37 Wo 2013

398.2/73/0946   2012951565

This series first published by:
Red Chair Press LLC   PO Box 333   South Egremont, MA 01258-0333

Printed in the United States of America

1 2 3 4 5 18 17 16 15 14

There once was a poor young girl who wandered the country begging for work. One day she came upon a thatched cottage where her luck turned.

"I need someone who can tend my cows. I'll give you a chance," said the farmer.

The girl proved her worth. Then one day she heard a groan near the meadow. She left the cows to graze and found a lion stretched upon the ground.

"Oh dear," she murmured. "You have a thorn in your foot. Quiet now. I'll pull it out."

After she removed the thorn, the lion licked her hand with his big rough tongue. She bound up his paw with her handkerchief.

The girl returned to the meadow, only to discover that the cows were gone. After searching for hours, she told the farmer the truth.

"How could you lose an entire herd of cows?" the farmer thundered. "I should send you away."

"Is there nothing else I can do?" she begged.

"I'll give you a week to look after the donkeys. Then we'll see if you are trustworthy," he said.

The young girl took the donkeys to graze every day. After a year, she found the same lion with a deep wound on his face. She cleaned his face, covered the wound with herbs, and bound it with her handkerchief. Once again, he licked her hand in thanks. And as before, the herd of donkeys was gone. She returned to face the farmer's wrath.

He scolded her, but he knew she had given him
a year of good service. "I'll give you one last
chance. Take the pigs out to forage. If you can
fatten them up, you can stay."

Another year passed, and the pigs grew fatter. But then she heard that familiar sound. She found her lion-friend gravely wounded. She washed each wound, gathered healing herbs, and tore her skirt for bandages. This time the lion spoke, "Won't you sit with me while I rest?"

"I'm sorry, but I must leave and tend to the farmer's pigs," she said.

She ran to find the pigs, but it was as if the
earth had swallowed them. After searching for
hours, she climbed a tree. Although she didn't
see the pigs, she did spy something startling.
A disheveled man walked down the path,
pulled aside a rock, and disappeared.

"Who was that?" the girl wondered. "I don't
dare go home to face the farmer's wrath, so I'll
just wait and see."

She dozed in the tree until the sun came up. Suddenly, the rock moved and the lion padded down the path.

"The lion!" the girl whispered. "Where did the man go?"

The girl slipped down from the tree, pushed aside the rock, and followed the path to a large room. She tiptoed inside. Finding plenty of food, she made herself a meal. Then she tidied up the food, swept, and dusted the room.

That evening, she watched from her tree until the man returned. The next morning, out came the lion. Again, she returned to the hidden room, made a meal, and tidied up. After several days, the girl waited for the man on the path.

"I thought it was you who was cleaning my place," he said.

"How do you know me? And why do you leave as a lion and return as a man?" she asked.

"I was enchanted by a giant who resented that I was a prince loved by the people. By day I am the lion you have helped," explained the man. "The giant stole your animals in revenge. The only way to break the spell is to give him a cloak made from a princess's lock of hair."

"Well, I'll go to the city and find work at the palace. I'll get that lock of hair," she promised.

The next day she fixed her hair carefully and walked to the palace calling, "Who will hire me?" The waiting-maid of the princess heard her. "What can you do?" she asked.

"I can make anyone's hair shine like gold," she responded.

"Then come with me," said the maid. Every day, the girl brushed the princess's hair until it gleamed like the sun.

One day, the girl worked up her courage and asked if she could have a lock of hair. The princess refused at first. But the girl begged until she gave in.

"You can have one lock of hair," said the princess, "if you find a handsome prince to make me happy."

The girl agreed, cut off the lock, and wove the hair into a coat that glittered like silk. She took it to the poor lion-man, who told her how to find the giant.

Hearing her climb the mountain, the giant rushed out with his sword in one hand and a club in the other.

"Wait! I've brought you a coat!" she called.

But the coat was too short and he threw it down.

"I'm sorry. I'll try again," she promised.

The next morning, the girl begged so hard that the princess let her have another lock. The girl made a bigger coat and returned to the mountain. This time the coat fit, and the giant offered a reward.

"Please break the spell on the lion-man," she begged.

The giant answered, "You must kill the lion.
Then burn him and cast his ashes on the water.
Then you will have your prince."

The girl wept as she told the man what
happened.

"Do as he said. Trust me," said the man.

The next morning the girl killed the lion. After she cast the ashes into the water, out came a handsome young prince.

"Thank you, dear one. You have saved me, and now I can ask you to be my wife."

The young girl looked at him through tears. "But I have promised the princess that I would find her a prince to make her happy."

The prince replied, "There is nothing to fear. You see, I am the king's son. She is my sister. Let us go to the palace now. Knowing her brother is home will bring her happiness."

The king, queen, and princess were delighted with the prince's return. The king, being grateful to the young girl for her devotion, consented to the marriage. And the whole city celebrated!

WORDS TO KNOW

consented: agreed to; gave permission for something to happen

disheveled: untidy or messy

enchanted: put under a spell

forage: search for food

thatched: made with a roof of straw, grass or reeds

wrath: extreme anger

Question 1: Each time the girl took care of the farmer's animals, they disappeared. Who took the animals? Why?

Question 2: Why did the girl go to town and find work in the palace? What was she trying to get?

Question 3: The girl promised the princess that she would find a prince to make her happy. Do you think she kept her promise? How?

About Spain

Spain's history is long and colorful. In the 1500s the royal rulers of Spain were among the most powerful in the world. During this period of the Habsburg monarchy, many kings and princes ruled over different regions of Spain. Our tale is from this time when many young people had dreams of marrying a wealthy prince or princess.

About the Author

After fifteen years as a teacher, Suzanne Barchers began a career in writing and publishing. She has written over 100 children's books and more than 20 reader's theater and teacher resource books. She previously held editorial roles at Weekly Reader and LeapFrog and is on the PBS Kids Media Advisory Board. Suzanne also plays the flute professionally – and for fun – from her home in Stanford, CA.

About the Illustrator

John Joven got his start as a graphic designer and illustrator when he was 8 years old. He shares his passion for drawing and painting with his wife and two children at home in Bogotá, Colombia.